MEET ALL THESE FRIENDS IN BUZZ BOOKS:

Thomas the Tank Engine
The Animals of Farthing Wood
Fireman Sam
Joshua Jones
Looney Tunes
Babar
Rupert
Flintstones
Bugs Bunny
James Bond Junior

This presentation first published in 1993 by Buzz Books,
an imprint of Reed Children's Books
Michelin House, 81 Fulham Road, London SW3 6RB
and Auckland, Melbourne, Singapore and Toronto

First published in Great Britain 1962 by
Methuen & Co Ltd
Copyright © Librairie Hachette 1961
This presentation copyright © 1993 Reed International Books
Limited

ISBN 1 85591 3135

Printed in Italy by LEGO

BABAR

and the Castle

LAURENT DE BRUNHOFF

Babar, the king of the elephants, had decided to move to Bonnetrompe Castle. All the furniture was packed into removal vans and Babar, Celeste and the family followed behind. It was a beautiful day.

6

As the car climbed the hill they could see the ancient turrets of the castle. The first removal van was too wide to go through the gate into the courtyard and had to be unloaded on the grass outside.

7

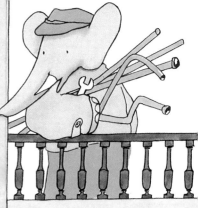

In the magnificent entrance hall the children admired the ancestral portraits.

"I like the musketeer," said Arthur.

"The Roman soldier is my favourite," said Zephir.

But Babar sighed when he saw the plumber. "What a nuisance. The work isn't finished yet."

As the decorator had plenty to do, Arthur offered to hang the wallpaper in his room himself. While Pom put a last coat of paint on the door, Flora spread the paste on the paper. Zephir perched on the stepladder to hang the paper on the wall, and Arthur held it up with his trunk. It wasn't easy.

When Pom had finished his painting, he tried his hand at plastering. Even his trunk got stuck in it! Just then Alexander came in, black as a sweep.

10

"Where have you been?" asked Zephir.

"In the cellars," said Alexander. "I was looking for the underground passage. Every castle has one somewhere."

Just then, Queen Celeste came in. She was cross when she saw how dirty they were.

"Go under the shower, quickly, and scrub yourselves hard with the brush. The bathroom is ready."

In the great dining hall, near a huge pile
of empty trunks, the old lady served the
soup. Pom had fallen asleep in a suitcase.

"Poor child," said the old lady. "He
worked too hard this afternoon. Wake him
gently, Zephir."

13

In the middle of the night, Alexander got out of bed and went to waken Pom and Flora.

"Let's go and look for the underground passage," he said.

In the next bedroom, Arthur and Zephir got up, too. Together they all crept through the castle and up to the top of the old tower where the owl lived.

Unfortunately, the owl had never heard of an underground passage. He advised them to visit the armoury, and showed them the way.

"Medieval armour!" exclaimed Arthur, when he finally found the light switch. "Just like in my history book at school."

Flora, Alexander and Zephir helped him to put on a marvellous suit of gilded armour.

Pom dressed up in a little suit of black armour and battle commenced. What a row they made! Swords clashed on breast-plates. The armour was heavy, and the two warriors were soon out of breath. When Arthur lost his balance and fell head over heels, they all shouted with laughter. But the noise of his fall resounded through the passages. BBRANG-CRRASSH. The children were terrified and rushed away.

Arthur and Pom got
out of the armour.

But Pom's foot
was stuck fast.

Back in his room,
he started to cry.

No one could get
the metal boot off.

First Arthur, then
Zephir, tried to
help him.

It was no good.
The spur came off
in Zephir's hand.

Pom dared not
disturb Babar, and
went to bed.

Next morning Babar
cut the boot off.

The whole family spent the day in the
castle grounds. With Pom's help, Flora
caught a goldfish in the ornamental pond.

"I shall keep it on my mantelpiece,"
she said.

20

Babar, seated on a splendid new motor-
mower, cut the lawns. Arthur raked up the
cut grass into heaps, and Zephir . . . was up
to no good.

Alexander decided to explore, and found a pavilion at the edge of the wood. Hearing him call, the others hurried to join him.

"Isn't it pretty?" said Flora, trotting towards the door.

"It's peaceful," added Arthur. "Couldn't we hold our club meetings here?"

"Let's see what is inside first," advised Zephir.

22

They managed to open the heavy door, and went into a gloomy room: a library filled with dusty books.

Alexander climbed the steps and rummaged everywhere. Just as he touched one of the little carved elephants' heads, a door swung open in the wall.

"The underground passage!" he shouted.

They found some candles and made their
way cautiously along the tunnel, their hearts
in their mouths, until –

they emerged through
the fireplace into the
drawing room of the
castle! Babar and
Celeste were amazed.
"A-A-Alexander?
What does this mean?"
demanded Celeste.

"They've found the
secret tunnel!" cried
Babar. "Bravo, children!"

25

Some days later, dozens of cars rolled into the courtyard of the castle and were parked in neat rows against the wall. King Babar and Queen Celeste were giving a castle-warming party at Bonnetrompe.

Babar and Celeste received their guests at the top of the steps, in their ceremonial robes. Professor and Mrs Fandago were there, Mrs Hatchibombotar and her children, Mr and Mrs Pilophage and many others.

The banqueting hall was full of happy
revellers. The children were wildly excited.
They gathered round the buffet. Zephir
grabbed a cherry tart. Arthur stretched his
trunk towards the chocolate éclairs.

28

The old lady sat down at the piano and,
with the trumpeter of the orchestra, set the
guests dancing. The party lasted till dawn,
long after the children had gone to bed, and
the castle windows were brilliant with
lights all night.

29